tickleOctopus

BY AUDREY WOOD

Illustrated by Bill Morrison

Houghton Mifflin Company Boston 1980

To Bruce Robert,
who taught me to see
with magic eyes

Library of Congress Cataloging in Publication Data

Wood, Audrey.
  Tickleoctopus.

  SUMMARY: Chaos abounds when a little boy, back from
puddle fishing, unleashes his merciless secret pet on
unsuspecting adults.
  I. Morrison, Bill, 1935- II. Title.
PZ7.W846Ti   [E]   79-22600
ISBN 0-395-29083-X

Don't tell me you're going puddle-fishing again.
Please! Try to keep your feet dry.

The rain is over, it's time to play.
Fishing, fishing is good today.

What are you fishing for, leaves and rocks?
Don't you know you can't catch anything
in a puddle?
Ha-ha, that is the most ridiculous thing
I've ever seen.

Hey, Son, this Saturday we'll go down to
the lake, and I'll show you some real fishing.

This is no place to be fishing, young man.
Sidewalks are for walking.

9

Hey, Dad. Want to see what I caught?

What is it, Son?

Oh...just a Tickleoctopus.

Hm-m-m. And what does a Tickleoctopus do?

Oh my . . . Hee-hee. That tickles!
I just can't stand it.
Ha-ha. Stop, please!

Come on, Tickle-O.

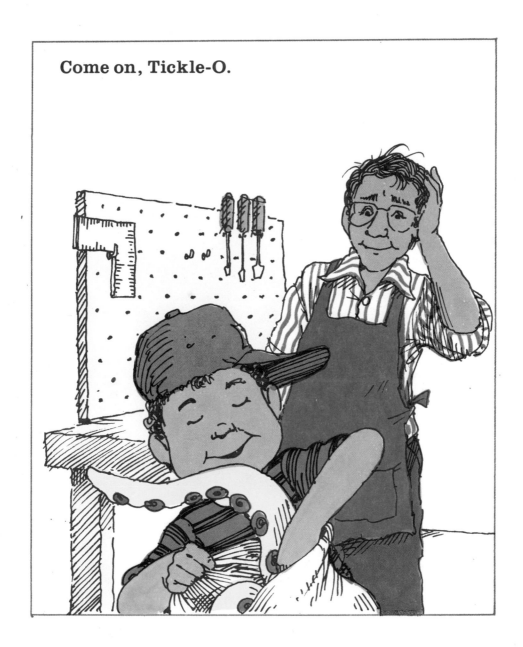

Hi, Mom. Want to see a Tickleoctopus?

Where have you been?
You know it's time to go shopping . . .
Well, if it won't
take long I suppose I might
as well have a peek.

Oh no! Stop! Ha-ha!
That tickles!

That Tickleoctopus certainly can tickle.
Does it ever tickle you?

Nope.

Hi, Charlie. The fishing was great.
Want to see what I caught in the puddle?

Come now, fun is fun, but you can't trick
old Charlie. Hand it on up here.

Oh my gosh! It tickles! Take it away.
Hee-hee. It really tickles!
Ho-ho-ho.

Whew! That's the best tickle
I've had in a long time.
What was it?

A Tickleoctopus.

Hop in, kid.
You and your Tickleoctopus
deserve a ride home.

Hi, Mrs. Bixler. Guess what?
The sidewalk is a good place to fish.
I caught a Tickleoctopus.
Want to see it?

Goodness me, it looks rather large.
Is it dangerous?

Nope. It's very friendly.

In that case, yes... I suppose so.

Oh no. It tickles!
It just tickles all over!
Oh you Tickleoctopus!

Time to go, Tickle-O.
Oh-oh. Look out, everybody!
The Tickleoctopus is loose!

Yipes! Run, run.
Let's get out of here!

Quick. Close the windows.

Well, now that the Tickleoctopus game is over,
how about some iced tea and a nice, long talk.

I can't remember playing a game I enjoyed
more than that one.

Make-believe is such fun,
and those tickles, they almost seemed real.

Don't children come up with the wildest ideas.
Oh well, it's time we got back to our work.
After all, there are more serious matters than . . .

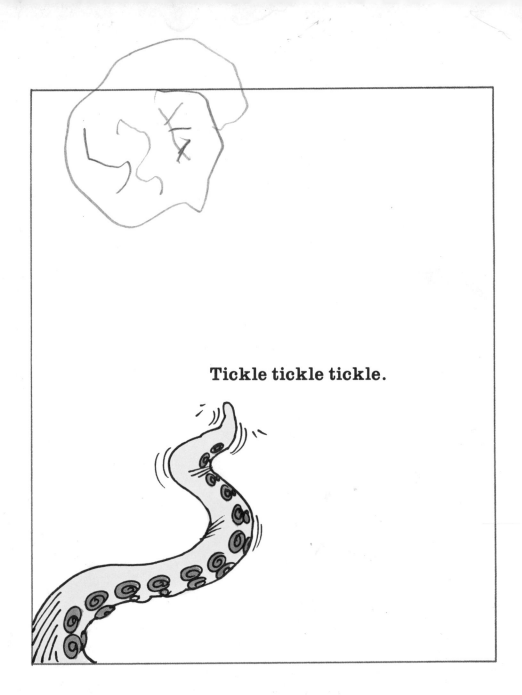

Tickle tickle tickle.